CURMUDGEON (kur-MUH-jun) n. A bad-tempered, difficult, cranky person; a grouch.

For Louisa and Charlie Cobb, and for Bruce Paterson
—M.B.

For Violet and Henry Vessey, with love
—F.W.

THIS IS A BORZOI BOOK PUBLISHED BY ALFRED A. KNOPF

Text copyright © 2019 by Matthew Burgess
Jacket art and interior illustrations copyright © 2019 by Fiona Woodcock

Visit us on the Web! rhcbooks.com

Educators and librarians, for a variety of teaching tools, visit us at RHTeachersLibrarians.com

Library of Congress Cataloging-in-Publication Data is available upon request.
ISBN 978-0-399-55662-3 (trade)—ISBN 978-0-399-55663-0 (lib. bdg.)—ISBN 978-0-399-55664-7 (ebook)

The text of this book is set in 16-point Bliss.
The illustrations were created with hand-cut rubber stamps, stencils, and children's blow pens,
with additional pencil line work, all composited digitally.

MANUFACTURED IN CHINA
March 2019
10 9 8 7 6 5 4 3 2 1

First Edition

THE UNBUDGEABLE CURMUDGEON

MATTHEW BURGESS

illustrated by
FIONA WOODCOCK

Alfred A. Knopf   New York

How do you budge
an unbudgeable curmudgeon
who really refuses to budge?

You might ask the curmudgeon
if he wouldn't mind scooching
over a smidgen.

Or you could distract the curmudgeon
by changing the subject. . . .

Maybe he's hungry?

You could offer the curmudgeon
a chunky wedge of your
peanut butter and jelly sandwich.

Chocolate fudge brownies
have been known to make
curmudgeons budge.

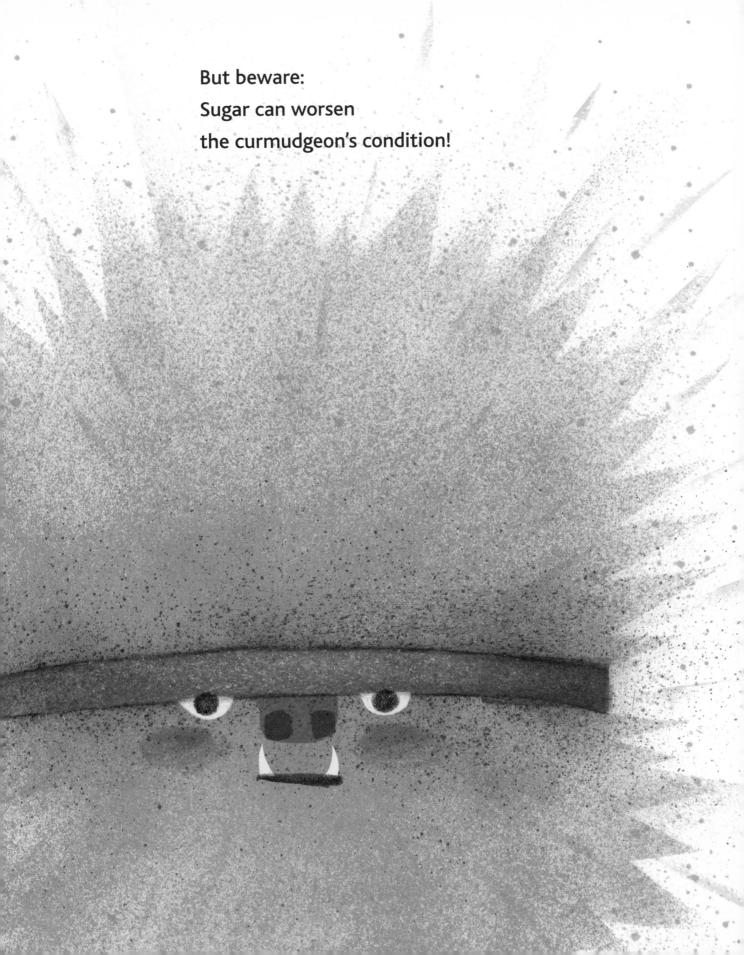

But beware:
Sugar can worsen
the curmudgeon's condition!

MOM!

You might try
getting the curmudgeon
in trouble.

Maybe that'll budge him!

Some say,
"If you can't budge 'em,
join 'em."

But where does that get you?

It wouldn't be right
to bludgeon the curmudgeon,

but maybe he *deserves*
one humongous nudge.

How do you budge
an unbudgeable curmudgeon
who really refuses to budge?

Hugs can budge curmudgeons . . .

. . . sometimes.

Reading a book
in a cozy nook can do the trick . . .

. . . or not.

If all else fails,
you can try turning on
a favorite song . . .

. . . the one that makes you
sing along.

It can be tricky
to get the gunk off
the funkiest funks,

but once a curmudgeon
begins to budge . . .

. . . you'd be surprised
how quickly . . .

the grouchiness can vanish!

For now . . .